MW00760767

White Thunder

Dave and Pat Sargent are longtime residents of Prairie Grove, Arkansas. Dave, a fourth-generation dairy farmer, began writing in early December of 1990, and Pat, a former teacher, began writing in the fourth grade. They enjoy the outdoors and have a real love for animals.

White Thunder

Animal Pride Series
Book 6

By

Dave and Pat Sargent

Beyond The End
By
Sue Rogers

Illustrated by
Jeane Lirley Huff

ERMA SIEGEL ELEMENTARY
135 W. THOMPSON LANE
MURFREESBORO, TN 37129

Ozark Publishing, Inc.
P.O. Box 228
Prairie Grove, AR 72753

Cataloging-in-Publication Data

Sargent, Dave, 1941-
   White Thunder / by Dave and Pat Sargent ; illustrated by Jeane Lirley Huff. —Prairie Grove, AR : Ozark Publishing, ©2003.
     ix, 36 p. : col. ill. ; 21 cm. (Animal pride series ; 6)
     "I'm a leader"—Cover.
   SUMMARY: White Thunder saves a herd of wild mustangs from capture by ranchers. Includes facts about the physical characteristics, behavior, and habitat of mustangs.
     ISBN: 1-56763-769-8 (hc)
           1-56763-770-1 (pbk)
     1. Mustang—Juvenile fiction. [1. Mustang—Fiction. 2. Horses—Fiction.] I. Sargent, Pat, 1936- II. Huff, Jeane Lirley, 1946- ill. III. Title. IV. Series: Sargent, Dave, 1941- Animal pride series ; 6.

   PZ10.3.S243Wh 2003
   [Fic]—dc21   96-001495

Factual information excerpted/adapted from
THE WORLD BOOK ENCYCLOPEDIA.
© World Book, Inc. By permission of the publisher.
www.worldbook.com
Copyright © 2003 by Dave and Pat Sargent
All rights reserved

Printed in the United States of America

iv

Inspired by

the free spirit and speed of wild mustangs we've seen from time to time while driving through a couple of the western states.

Dedicated to

all boys and girls who love to ride horses.

Foreword

From the very moment the little white mustang was born, there was something about him that set him apart from the other horses. Like his father, White Thunder was truly a natural-born leader.

Contents

If you would like to have the authors of the Animal Pride Series visit your school, free of charge, call 1-800-321-5671 or 1-800-960-3876.

One

White Thunder

It was spring and the mares were in foal. One morning, Minnie Mae gave birth to a colt. She called him White Thunder, for he was like the peaks of the snow-covered mountains.

From the time White Thunder was born, he could run faster than any of the other colts. While the colts and fillies were growing up, they were always racing each other, and White Thunder won every race. He was a very high-spirited, proud colt and a natural-born leader. Minnie Mae and the other horses felt that White Thunder would one day rule over a big herd of wild mustangs.

That fall when White Thunder was a little over eight months old, the mares started leaving the colts and fillies for several days at a time, for they were now old enough to be on their own. Wherever the colts and fillies went, White Thunder was always in the lead. It was obvious that the wild mustang was a natural leader.

One day while the herd was moving from one valley to another, they ran into several men on horses. The herd whirled and ran in another direction. They wanted to stay far away from the men on horseback. They didn't know they were running into a trap.

White Thunder's dad was the leader of the herd and he could only think about leading his herd to safety. But every time he led the herd in a different direction, there were more men on horseback waiting for them. Now, White Thunder's dad realized that they were being forced into a blind canyon, and he knew that there was no way out.

Once the wild mustangs were in the blind canyon, they were driven into corrals and were broken to ride.

A few of the horses were sold to ranchers and many were sold to the army.

White Thunder's dad could not be broken to ride. The men who had captured the wild mustangs finally realized that White Thunder's dad would only cause them problems, so they released him, and he went back to the wide-open range.

Two

"They'll Never Ride Me!"

All the young colts and fillies, including White Thunder, were taken to a ranch and put in a pasture with high fences all around it. There was no escape.

When White Thunder and the others were two years old, they were put into a corral. The rancher and one of the cowboys began breaking the horses to ride. White Thunder said, "They'll never ride me!"

One by one, the young horses were broken to ride. Each time the

men roped White Thunder, he would
buck and jump and run and fight.

When they placed a saddle on his back, he would fall to the ground and would not get up until the saddle was removed.

Finally, all the young horses were broken to ride—all except White Thunder. He still refused to be ridden.

White Thunder was now alone in the pasture and was getting very lonesome. He sometimes stood for hours and gazed at the mountains, remembering the good times he'd had when he was free.

White Thunder decided that he would practice jumping every day until he could jump high enough to clear the tall fence around the big pasture.

So every day, the wild mustang ran as fast as he could run and jumped as high as he could jump, and each time, he knew that he had jumped a little higher than the time before.

The day finally came when White Thunder said, "I know I can clear the tall fence. I'll wait until tomorrow so I'll be rested and fresh."

The next morning at first light, White Thunder walked over to the tall fence and stood gazing at the mountains on the other side. He turned and trotted to the other end of the pasture, then wheeled and ran toward the fence as fast as he could run. Just as he reached the fence, he lunged upward with all his might. His front feet cleared the fence, but his chest made contact with it. His jump was too short, and he knew that he wasn't going to make it over.

As White Thunder fell backward, his back hoof caught between two boards in the fence. He kicked and jerked.

White Thunder finally managed to get free, but his foot was hurting so badly, he couldn't put his weight on it. He limped around for several days before his foot started feeling better. Day by day he was able to put more weight on it, but a month had passed before he could run at all.

Little by little, White Thunder got his strength back. He ran every day, not far at first, but every day he ran a little farther until he was able to run as fast as he ever could.

One morning when he awoke, White Thunder stood gazing at the mountains and a feeling of sadness came over him. He was tired of being alone. He missed his friends and wanted to be with other horses. He said to himself, "Today I will try to jump the fence again."

White Thunder started running around the pasture to loosen his powerful muscles. When he felt the time was right, he ran toward the tall fence, faster and harder than he had ever run in his life.

When he got near the fence, he unleashed all the power in his body. With a mighty jump, the mustang sailed upward, barely clearing the tall fence.

White Thunder landed on the ground on the other side. He was free!

Three

Free at Last

White Thunder headed straight for the tall mountains where he hoped to find some of his friends. He ran and ran in search of a herd of wild mustangs.

He had searched for a week before he finally located a small herd of wild mustangs. There were about fifty of them. As he moved in to join them he was met by a big black stallion. The black stallion said, "I am the leader of this herd and you are not welcome."

White Thunder turned and walked away. He climbed to the top of a nearby hill and stood watching the herd for a long time.

As the herd of mustangs moved away, White Thunder followed at a distance. Then, suddenly, he sensed danger. He looked around and saw men on horseback. He knew that they were going to herd the wild mustangs into the blind canyon up ahead. He whinnied and took off running as fast as he could run!

White Thunder caught up with the herd and tried to persuade them to follow him, but they were faithful to their leader and would not take orders from anyone else. He raced over to the black stallion and reared up, challenging him for the right to be the leader.

The stallions fought for a long time. White Thunder reared, showing his teeth. The old leader lowered his head, accepting defeat, and moved slowly to the back of the herd.

White Thunder was now in charge. He knew the mustangs would follow his commands. He knew what the riders were trying to do. They were trying to herd the wild mustangs into the blind canyon where they had trapped his dad's herd when White Thunder was a young colt.

White Thunder tossed his head and gave a loud whinny. His herd was surrounded and he realized that their only escape was for him to lead them right through the middle of the riders. He also knew that the wild mustangs were afraid of the riders and wanted to stay as far away from them as they could.

White Thunder reared up and neighed, commanding his herd to follow him. He took off straight for the riders. The mustangs started after him but stopped. Sensing their fear, White Thunder again reared and neighed, commanding them to follow him.

The wild mustangs had always trusted their leader. They responded to the command and ran toward White Thunder. He wheeled and led them straight toward the riders.

When the riders realized that White Thunder and his herd were coming straight toward them, they were afraid of getting trampled, so they turned and took off at a gallop.

White Thunder knew that he had saved the mustangs from certain capture. He thought, "I am in charge of a herd of wild mustangs. This is something that I've always wanted, but I know that being a leader means responsibility. I am responsible for my herd. I have to find good pasture for them. I also have to keep them safe from wild animals such as mountain lions and bears. I'll have to find a warm place for them to spend the cold nights."

None of these things would be a problem for White Thunder, for he was a natural-born leader.

That evening, White Thunder led the herd into a fertile valley full of lush, green grass. The valley was surrounded by hills which would protect them from cold winter winds.

The herd settled down and started grazing. White Thunder made his way to the top of a nearby hill where he could keep watch over his domain. He reared up and gave a long neigh, proclaiming his rule over the valley and his herd of mustangs.

Four

Mustang Facts

The Mustang is a small wild horse that inhabits the western United States. A mustang averages only about fourteen hands in height and weighs from six hundred to eight hundred pounds. It is swift, sure-footed, tough, and intelligent. It is well suited to conditions on the Great Plains. Mustangs descended from escaped Indian horses, which in turn were descended from horses brought to the New World by the Spanish about 1500.

As the West was being settled, mustangs were tamed and used as cow ponies. In the mid-seventeenth century they numbered from two to four million. Today only around twenty thousand are found, most of them in the West.

The Pony Express horses were not thoroughbreds. They were very tough healthy little wild mustangs or Indian ponies.

None of these wild mustangs weighed more than a thousand pounds, all had extremely hard hoofs, and most of them had little training. One Pony Express station keeper claimed a horse was ready for use "when a rider could lead it out of the station without getting his head kicked off." On horseback these express riders carried the mail across the scorching Nevada wastelands and through Rocky Mountain passes, where the snow was sometimes as much as thirty-two feet deep.

The Plains Indians used the Mustang to hunt buffalo. The horses were often gored, and riders were frequently thrown or trampled. The hardworking buffalo horse provided Plains Indians with the necessities of life, but sometimes the price was high.

While Indian horses hunted buffalo, there were other animals who hunted treasure. In the sixteenth century Spanish prospectors came to America to search for gold and silver, and horses helped them dig these precious metals out of the earth.

The horses powered hoists and pumps. They dragged heavy stones across the metal-bearing ore to crush it into powder. In the New World horses often had one other special job: they helped extract gold.

A century ago there were some two million of these wild horses roaming the western plains. Settlers and Indians tamed thousands, and as cattle horses, war-horses, buffalo horses, and workhorses, they helped build the West.

In the twentieth century, however, American ranchers don't tame mustangs. They shoot them because wild horses eat the grass intended for sheep and cattle. By 1971 so many wild mustangs had been killed that Congress passed a law to keep them from being hunted to extinction. Thanks to that legislation, some wild horses still race through the back country in many western states, but the herds are smaller now. In 1983 government officials estimated there were only about forty-five thousand mustangs left.

The United States government's Bureau of Land Management has found a way to save these horses. Instead of shooting mustangs to keep the herds down to a reasonable size, they periodically round up a number

of these wild mustangs and put them
up for adoption.

BEYOND "THE END"

LANGUAGE LINKS

Using the following vocabulary words:

Mustang	Responsibility
Stallion	Leader
Corral	Herd
Foal	Colt
Neigh	Blind canyon
Trot	Pasture
Challenge	Fillies
Domain	Obvious
Whinny	Trample
Gallop	Mare
Grazè	

1. Draw a circle around words for a horse.

2. Draw a rectangle around words that tell sounds horses make.

3. Draw a triangle around words that tell where horses are kept.

4. Draw a line under words that tell what horses sometimes do.

5. Look up the meanings of remaining words.

CURRICULUM CONNECTIONS

Find the height and weight of a mustang. (HINT: Look in the back of the book under Mustang Facts.) Students and teacher trace outline of their left hand, keeping thumb folded inside palm and fingers close together. Measure the width of one student's hand and compare it to the width of teacher's hand. Would the height of fourteen teacher's hands be the same as fourteen student's hands? No! So, just remember that men's hands average 4" wide. This was the original measurement used. By placing one hand on the ground, the other above it and moving the first hand over the second the horse could be measured from the ground to the withers. (Look up "withers" in the dictionary.)

Knowing this information, tape outline of hands on the classroom wall to equal 4 inches X 14. This is the average height of a wild mustang! How many hands did it take? Remember, it would only take 14 men's hands. How many more of your hands did it take?

Now borrow some scales from the school nurse. Students line up and weigh themselves. Add weights together to see how many classmates it takes to equal the weight of one mustang.

THE ARTS

Draw and color a picture of a mustang you would like to own. What would you name your horse?
Below the picture, write how it would feel to be riding your mustang through a green valley. Describe how the wind feels in your hair, the sounds you hear, and the speed and excitement of the ride.

THE BEST I CAN BE

White Thunder showed characteristics of being a leader from the day he was born. Working together, make a list of White Thunder's leadership characteristics. Do you feel that you have some of the same characteristics? Make a list of things about yourself that remind you of some of White Thunder's leadership characteristics. Visit the following web site for more information about mustangs: <www.blm.gov/whb> If you appreciate the efforts being made to protect the wild mustangs, write a thank-you letter to:

    Secretary of Interior
    U. S. Department of the Interior
    1849 C. Street N. W.
    Washington, DC 20240